TELL ME ABOUT:

UNESCO

The designations employed and the presentation of material throughout this publication do not imply the expression of any opinion whatsoever on the part of UNESCO concerning the legal status of any country, territory, city or area or of its authorities, or concerning the delimitation of its frontiers or boundaries.

Published in 2001 by the United Nations Educational,
Scientific and Cultural Organization,
7, place de Fontenoy,
75352 Paris 07 SP (France)

Translated from French: *Raconte-moi l'UNESCO*
(UNESCO Publishing/Nouvelle Arche de Noé Édition)
Edition Nouvelle Arche de Noé: layout and illustrations
UNESCO Publishing: texts and photos

ISBN 92-3-103802-8

TELL ME ABOUT:

UNESCO

Text Frédéric Bosc

UNESCO Publishing

'If all the people of the world were to hold hands, they could dance around the world.'

UNESCO was founded after the Second World War in order to construct 'the defences of peace' in the minds of men. For, if peace is to exist, it must first of all be desired by the women and the men of the whole world. But before that idea takes shape in the minds of each one of us, a long road remains to be travelled. Now it is up to you, the children of today, to form a circle about the earth in order to build a joyful world where peace will reign throughout.

Children can greatly affect the course of things: they look to others, see how they live, understand them and love them, stand by them in their fights for good causes. So I invite you to join your forces and your enthusiasms and take up our many challenges: discover, cherish and safeguard the cultures of the world, defend human rights, care for the environment, protect endangered species...

Why not start by launching activities at school, among friends or at home, and put your imagination at the service of a grand design: make our planet more beautiful, create a haven of peace and happiness for all. It can be a thrilling adventure, it will not be easy, but it will certainly be worth trying.

I hope that this little book, which tells the story of UNESCO, its tasks and its great achievements, may help to inspire you and, maybe, give you a few ideas.

KOICHIRO MATSUURA
Director-General of UNESCO

What is UNESCO?

To maintain peace and security in all corners of the world is the purpose and principle of the United Nations. Several institutions within the system attempt to dissuade States from waging war or try at least to contain the havoc wreaked by such conflicts. The role of UNESCO is to prevent* strife from arising at all: the Organization wants 'to contribute to peace and security in the world by promoting collaboration among the nations through education, science and culture'.

● *The background*

As early as 1942, in wartime, the governments of the European countries which were confronting Nazi Germany and its allies met in the United Kingdom. The Second World War was far from over, yet those countries were looking for ways and means to reconstruct their systems of education once peace was restored. Very quickly, the project gained momentum and soon took on a universal note. New governments, including that of the United States, decided to join in.

In 1945, Paris was chosen to host UNESCO. After a brief sojourn in temporary premises, the Organization moved into new buildings, constructed in the seventh arrondissement, in 1958.

* *Words followed by an asterisk (*) are explained in the Glossary, p. 45.*

Scarcely had the war ended when an important conference opened in London, on 1 November 1945. It gathered together the representatives of some forty countries. Spurred on by France and the United Kingdom, two countries that had known great hardship during the conflict, the delegates decided to create an organization that would embody a genuine culture of peace. In their eyes, the new organization must establish the 'intellectual and moral solidarity of mankind' and, in so doing, prevent the outbreak of another world war.

On 16 November 1945, thirty-seven countries signed the Constitution, thus marking the birth of the United Nations Educational, Scientific and Cultural Organization (UNESCO). The Constitution came into force in 1946 after ratification by twenty countries: Australia, Brazil, Canada, China, Czechoslovakia, Denmark, Dominican Republic, Egypt, France, Greece, India, Lebanon, Mexico, New Zealand, Norway, Saudi Arabia, South Africa, Turkey, United Kingdom, United States. These were the first States Signatory to the Constitution.

Why education?

A farmer will be able to read the instructions for the use of the fertilizer he spreads on his fields, he will know what price he can ask for his produce, he will be able to count the animals in his herds and flocks.

A mother will be able to read her children's vaccination card, give them encouragement and help them with their homework. She will be able to learn about nutrition and health, sell the fruit of her labours and obtain a small loan.

A girl will marry a little later (not at twelve or fifteen, as has sometimes been the case) and will have fewer children than before.

The population will be able to use its judgement, know its rights, develop its potential, read the newspaper and take part in the life of the country.

The Constitution

In the introduction – called the Preamble – the Constitution of UNESCO declares that 'since wars begin in the minds of men, it is in the minds of men that the defences of peace must be constructed'. It also declares that 'ignorance of each other's ways and lives has been a common cause, throughout the history of mankind, of that suspicion and mistrust between the peoples of the world, through which their differences have all too often broken into war'.

So that a unanimous, lasting and genuine peace may be secured, the Preamble declares that the States Signatory to the Constitution 'believing in full and equal opportunities for education for all, in the unrestricted pursuit of objective truth and in the free exchange of ideas and knowledge, are agreed and determined to develop and to increase the means of communication between their peoples and to employ these means for the purpose of mutual understanding and a truer and more perfect knowledge of each other's lives'.

In order to achieve that aim, the States concerned decided to found 'the United Nations Educational, Scientific and Cultural Organization for the purpose of advancing, through the educational, scientific and cultural relations of the peoples of the world, the objectives of international peace and of the common welfare of mankind for which the United Nations Organization was established and which its Charter proclaims'.

The emblem of UNESCO was adopted in 1954. It recalls the temple of the Parthenon, erected on the hill of the Acropolis, in Athens. Thus it pays tribute to Greece where the idea of democracy was born in the sixth century B.C. Greek philosophical thought has left a very deep imprint on the whole of the Mediterranean basin.

Article One of the Constitution goes on to state that UNESCO, 'by promoting collaboration among the nations through education, science and culture' seeks to further 'universal respect for justice, for the rule of law and for the human rights and fundamental freedoms which are affirmed for the peoples of the world, without distinction of race, sex, language or religion'.

UNESCO belongs to what is called the UNITED NATIONS SYSTEM At the heart of this network is the United Nations Organization (UNO), which has its headquarters in New York (United States). A large number of intergovernmental institutions or programmes operate under the system around the world. Along with UNESCO, the best known are:

- The International Monetary Fund (IMF), established to promote international monetary co-operation and orderly exchange arrangements.

- The United Nations High Commissioner for Refugees (UNHCR), established to provide protection and assistance to refugees, who are people who have fled their homelands because of war or persecutions.

- The World Trade Organization (WTO) is the only international organization dealing with the global rules of trade between nations.

- The World Health Organization (WHO) helps all people to attain the highest possible level of health.

- The United Nations Children's Fund (UNICEF) helps governments, communities and families make the world a better place for children

- The Food and Agriculture Organization (FAO) works to decrease poverty and hunger by promoting agricultural development and a higher living standard in rural areas.

BECAUSE war kills ordinary people, not just soldiers: 90% of victims are civilians, quite often children and their mothers.

BECAUSE war destroys infrastructure: roads, schools, hospitals, buildings and houses.

BECAUSE war destroys the economy of countries: it is no longer a matter of producing, but of surviving.

Why peace ?

BECAUSE war is expensive; it means that national governments cannot spend their budgets on sectors which would be useful to the population, such as health, education or development.

BECAUSE war takes its toll on minds and hearts: those who have been harmed by violence or have witnessed torture or murder are seriously traumatized and, if not given special care, are at risk of being swept along on a growing tide of violence.

● Member States

By 1950, UNESCO counted fifty-nine Member States. In 1954, the USSR became the seventieth. Between 1960 and 1962, as a result of the decolonization process, twenty-four newly created African States were admitted. But in 1984, UNESCO lost an important member when the United States, who criticized both management and orientations, decided to leave the Organization. Shortly afterwards, the United Kingdom and Singapore followed suit.

From 1990 onwards, the dislocation of the Eastern block brought more changes. The seat of former East Germany was annulled with German reunification. A little later, the disintegrating USSR ceded its place to the Russian Federation. Twelve new Member States emerged from the collapse and, likewise, made their entry into UNESCO (these included Armenia, Azerbaijan, Georgia, Kazakhstan and Kyrgyzstan). Next, it was the turn of countries from the former Yugoslavia (Bosnia-Herzegovina, Croatia and Slovenia).

At the end of 2001, UNESCO comprised 188 Member States and six Associate Members* (Aruba, Netherlands Antilles, Cayman Islands, British Virgin Islands, Macao and Tokelau).

Since the foundation of UNESCO, ten Member States have withdrawn at one moment or another (South Africa, for example, left the Organization in 1956 to rejoin in 1994, after abolishing the system of apartheid*). All have returned with the exception of the United States of America and Singapore (the United Kingdom became a Member once more in 1997).

UNESCO Headquarters

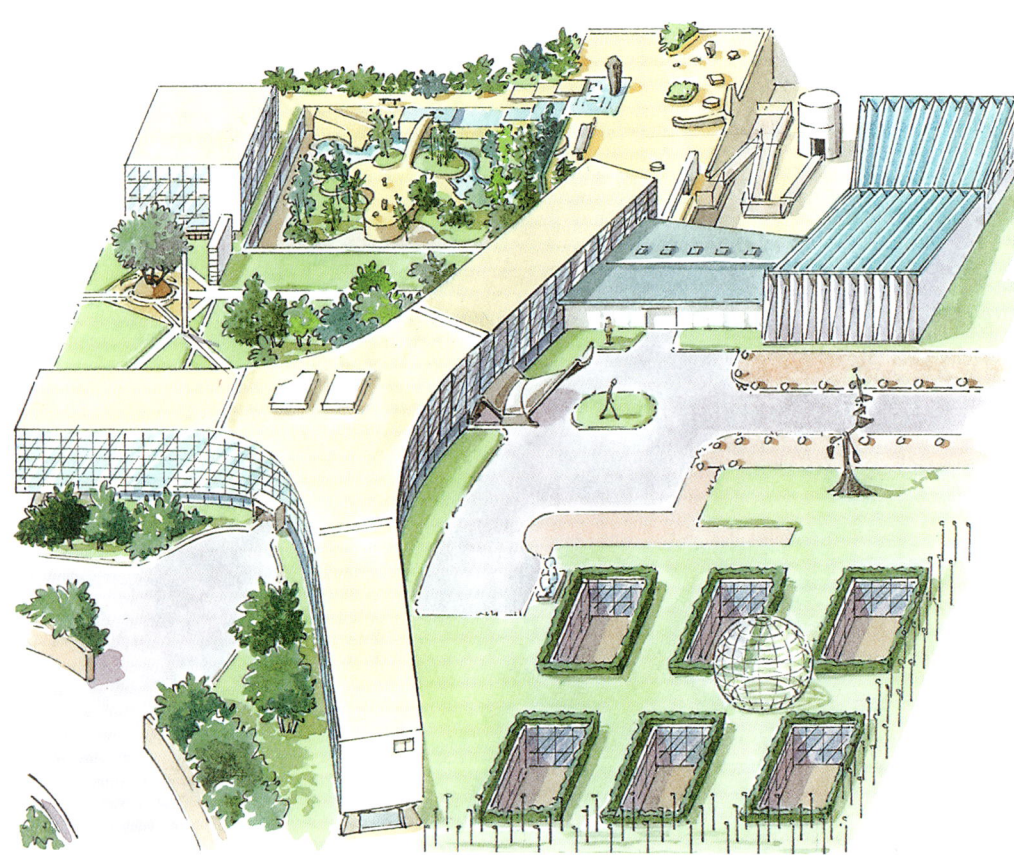

In the early years of its existence, UNESCO was installed in the Majestic, a large disused hotel near the Champs-Élysées, in central Paris. Staff were obliged to work from the rooms formerly reserved for guests and to keep their files in the bath-tubs!

Located in the Place de Fontenoy, in Paris, the main building which houses the Headquarters of UNESCO was inaugurated on 5 November 1958. The Y-shaped design was invented by three architects of different nationalities under the direction of an international committee. Nicknamed the 'three-pointed star', the entire edifice stands on seventy-two columns of concrete piling. It is world famous, not only because it is the home of a well-known organization but also because of its outstanding architectural qualities. Three more buildings complete the headquarters site.

The second building, known affectionately as the 'accordion', holds the egg-shaped hall with a pleated copper ceiling where the plenary sessions of the General Conference are held. The third building is in the form of a cube. Lastly, a fourth construction consists of two office floors hollowed out below street level, around six

small sunken courtyards. The buildings, which contain many remarkable works of art, are open to the public.

As soon as the architectural plans for of the site at the Place de Fontenoy had been approved, UNESCO commissioned a number of great artists to create works which would embellish the future premises. In some cases, the works are also intended to evoke the peace which the institution has sought to establish and preserve throughout the world. Over the years, other works were acquired. Some have been donated to the Organization by various Member States.

Some of the art works are areas, such as the *Garden of Peace* designed by the Japanese Isamu Noguchi. A stream, a pool, a traditional bridge, cherry trees, bamboos, magnolias

In addition to modern works, a large number of antique paintings and sculptures decorate the walls of UNESCO headquarters in Paris: a Cambodian divinity made between the twelfth and thirteenth centuries, several Roman mosaics, a pyrographic design on cowhide from Burkina Faso, Egyptian and Chinese statues, and a Peruvian shroud.

and flowers, as well as stones chosen from a Japanese island for their beautiful shape form a miniature landscape where one may go to meditate. The tallest stone is called the Fountain of Peace. The word 'peace' is engraved in Japanese characters in reverse. To read it, one must study its reflection in the pond.

13

Another garden, *Tolerance Square*, was created by the Israeli Dani Karavan. It was inaugurated in 1996 and dedicated to the Prime Minister of Israel, Yitzak Rabin, assassinated the previous year by an Israeli extremist. The centre of the square is dominated by an ancient olive tree. Not far from the tree, the symbol of peace, is a stone wall where the first lines of the Preamble to the Constitution of UNESCO are engraved in ten languages.

Halfway between architecture and sculpture, the *Meditation Space* was conceived by the Japanese Tadao Ando. This one-storey cylindrical structure is paved with granite flagstones which became radioactive when an atomic bomb exploded over Hiroshima on 6 August 1945. The stones have been decontaminated. This work was commissioned to commemorate the fiftieth anniversary of the Constitution in 1995.

Several sculptures adorn areas both inside and outside the buildings. *Spiral,* by the American Alexander Calder, is a mobile, ten metres high, which the slightest breath of wind sets in motion. In a somewhat similar artistic vein, *Aeolian Signals* by the Greek Vassilakis Takis, given to UNESCO by Greece in 1993, symbolizes windmills of varying size and colour. *Walking Man* by the Swiss Alberto Giacometti, an extremely slender silhouette measuring 1.83 metres, is an allegory of the human being intent on claiming the universe. In total contrast,

the imposing *Reclining Figure,* by the British artist Henry Moore, shows generous rounded volumes. The *Symbolic Globe* by the Dane Erik Reitzel, an enormous sphere of latticed aluminium, enshrining another much smaller sphere suspended at the centre, recalls the logo of the United Nations. The *Angel of Nagasaki* is espe-

cially moving: this head, framed by two wings, was brought from the church of Urakami, ruined in the explosion of the atomic bomb on Nagasaki on 9 August 1945. It was donated by the Japanese city to commemorate the thirtieth anniversary of UNESCO in 1976.

Picasso, Bazaine, Miró, Tapiès, Le Corbusier and many other artists, both renowned or unknown, all have their place in this universal museum that echoes the diversity of artistic creation throughout the world.

How does UNESCO work?

• *The General Conference*

The General Conference is the sovereign organ of UNESCO. It brings together the representatives of the Member States and meets every two years. Its duty is to set the programmes and the budget of the Organization. Each country has one vote, irrespective of its size or the extent of its contribution to the budget. Observers from certain non-member countries or from other international bodies may attend the debates.

The working languages of the General Conference are English, Arabic, Chinese, Spanish, French and Russian: the speeches of Member States are simultaneously translated into six languages as the debates proceed.

The first session of the General Conference was held at the Sorbonne, in Paris, in November–December 1946. The writer François Mauriac, the actor Louis Jouvet, the writer and statesman Leopold Sédar Senghor and the physicist Frédéric Joliot-Curie were members of the French Delegation.

INTERPRETERS

UNESCO's General Conference in Mexico City, Mexico, in 1947

The Executive Board

The Executive Board, in a sense, assures the overall management of UNESCO. It prepares the work of the General Conference and sees that its decisions are properly carried out. Its fifty-eight members are elected by the General Conference. The choice of these representatives is largely a matter of the diversity of the cultures and their geographical origin. Skilful negotiations may be needed before a balance is reached among the different regions of the world in a way that will reflect the universality of the Organization. The Executive Board meets twice a year.

The Secretariat and the Director-General

A new Director-General is elected every six years by the General Conference. Under his authority, the Secretariat is expected to translate into reality the programmes approved by the General Conference. In the early 1980s, staff members numbered almost 3,500 (just under 2,400 of whom worked at the Headquarters of the Organization in Paris, the rest being attached to UNESCO Offices in other parts of the world). In 2001, the Secretariat employed 1,800 civil servants, both executive and non-executive. Two-thirds work at Headquarters.

The present Director-General of UNESCO, who was elected in 1999, is the Japanese Koïchiro Matsuura.

The Offices away from Headquarters

UNESCO is represented by Field Offices in the five continents. Their role is to co-ordinate the work of the Organization at the regional level.

From 1946 to 1999, eight Directors-General have been elected at UNESCO. In chronological order: British citizen Julian Huxley, the Mexican Jaime Torres Bodet, John W. Taylor then Luther Evans (both citizens of the United States), the Italian Vittorino Veronese, the Frenchman René Maheu, the Senegalese Amadou-Mahtar M'Bow and the Spaniard Federico Mayor Zaragoza.

UNESCO FIELD OFFICE IN PHNOM PENH, CAMBODIA

• Subsidiary Organs

Since the creation of UNESCO, about one hundred consultative committees, international commissions and intergovernmental councils have been set up to carry out specific tasks or for purposes of reflection. In particular, they have considered the technical needs of the press, radio and cinema (1947–49), the scientific and cultural development of mankind (1950–69), education for the twenty-first century (Delors Commission, 1992–99), culture and development (Perez de Cuellar Commission (1992–99) and the ethics of scientific and technical knowledge (1998). These studies, based on reflection and research, contribute towards guiding UNESCO policies.

Did you know?

In 2000, the chief purchasers of books, records, photographic equipment, video and radio equipment, televisions, games and sports articles were the United States of America, Hong Kong, China, Canada and Australia.

 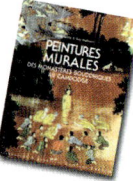   

• National Commissions

Most Member States and Associate Members of UNESCO have formed a UNESCO National Commission in their own country. Today, there are 2,189 such structures, which have no equivalent within the United Nations system. The National Commissions are made up of intellectuals, academics and scientists and help to evolve, implement and evaluate UNESCO programmes. They send out information about the Organization by preparing publications and documents, holding exhibitions or organizing lectures. They also play an advisory role to their respective governments and pass on the ideas of the Organization.

The first National Commission was set up by Brazil in 1946.

The National Commissions form an essential link between the world of research and UNESCO. They entertain close relations with the Secretariat, both at Headquarters and at the Field Offices outside Paris. UNESCO regularly arranges meetings for those in charge, at the regional or interregional level, so as to be better informed about needs in the field.

☀ *Associated Schools*

The Associated Schools Project (ASP) was launched by UNESCO in 1953. The institutions belonging to this network endeavour to educate young people in a spirit of tolerance and international understanding, through teaching methods based on enlisting the active participation of the pupils themselves. Today, there are more than 6,700 Associated Schools spread over 65 countries. The number is steadily increasing. The Associated Schools are not administered by UNESCO. They form part of the system of education in their respective countries and enjoy no special status. But they are selected by the national authorities of each country. Their purpose is to act singly or as a group (at the local, national or international level) by developing pilot projects on four main themes:

GORKI ELEMENTARY SCHOOL, NANTERRE (FRANCE)

- global problems and the role of the United Nations system
- human rights, democracy and tolerance
- multicultural apprenticeship
- environmental problems.

☀ *UNESCO associations, centres and clubs*

The associations, centres and clubs are groups of individuals of all ages and from all social and professional walks of life. They share a common desire to uphold the values put forward by UNESCO. In consequence, they seek to make the Organization better known and carry out activities along the lines of those directly implemented by UNESCO. Like the National Commissions, they too, in a sense, serve as havens for the ideals of the Organization.

● Partnerships

UNESCO works in partnership with other United Nations international agencies. In addition, it maintains official relations of co-operation with 588 non-governmental organizations (NGOs*), and can rely upon more informal contacts with 1,200 sorts of organizations. This means that common undertakings can be carried out worldwide in all of UNESCO's fields of activity.

UNESCO may support the activities of an NGO in a shanty town in Dakar, for example, by drilling a well, installing latrines and street fountains, or introducing refuse collection. Everything is organized and managed by the population, which feels responsible for its own health and environment. The Organization may encourage women to form groups where they can receive training, and may also grant small loans (called 'micro-credit') to enable them to engage in occupations which will allow them to earn a little money: small trading, making satchels and sundry articles, or opening a community shop that they look after by themselves.

● Goodwill Ambassadors

Contrary to what their title might lead one to believe, Goodwill Ambassadors are not real diplomats. They are persons who, by their professional or other achievements, have gained international recognition. On account of their celebrity, UNESCO entrusts them with the task of promoting its missions and principles with a view to arousing as wide an interest as possible.

Among the 'Ambassadors', are footballer player Pelé, the racing car champion Michael Schumacher, actresses Catherine Deneuve and Claudia Cardinale, composer Jean-Michel Jarre and the violinist Yehudi Menuhin. There is even an astronaut, Patrick Baudry, as well as the Nobel Peace-prize laureat Rigoberta Menchu, the Guatemalan who defended the cause of the indigenous Mayan people, sorely tried by a civil war that has ravaged their country for decades.

RIGOBERTA MENCHU TUM IN GUATEMALA

NOMINATION OF JEAN-MICHEL JARRE AS GOODWILL AMBASSADOR

UNESCO budget

Did you know?

For an inhabitant of Bangladesh, a computer costs the equivalent of eight years of his or her salary; for an average American, one month of salary.

NEWSPAPER VENDOR, MADAGASCAR

Did you know?

The money spent on 10 stealth bombers, would provide 4 years of elementary schooling for 135 million out-of-school children

UNESCO can draw upon two types of financial resources. One source comes from the ordinary budget, which comprises the contributions paid by the Member States. These are calculated according to the economic strength of each country. In 2000, the poorest countries (they number about 40) each contributed 0.001% of the funds collected. At the other end of the scale, fewer than a dozen contries contribute more than 2% of the total budget. With contributions amounting to 25% of the ordinary budget, Japan has become the main financial backer* of the Organization.

For the 2-year period 2000–2001, the ordinary budget totalled US$544 million, a comparatively modest sum in the light of the funds available to other international organizations such as UNICEF or the UNHCR, both of which have a budget four times larger than UNESCO's.

The second source of money for UNESCO comes from extrabudgetary funds. For the financial year 2000–2001, these amounted to approximately US$250 million, US$113 million being the funds which Member States entrust to UNESCO to enable the Organization to undertake projects in the developing countries. Over US$60 million derive from the UN Development Programme (UNDP) or from United Nations agencies active in the areas of development, population, childhood or the environment, which share the same objectives as UNESCO.

OUTDOOR SCHOOL, MALAISIA

Where UNESCO's money comes from (for 2000, in %)

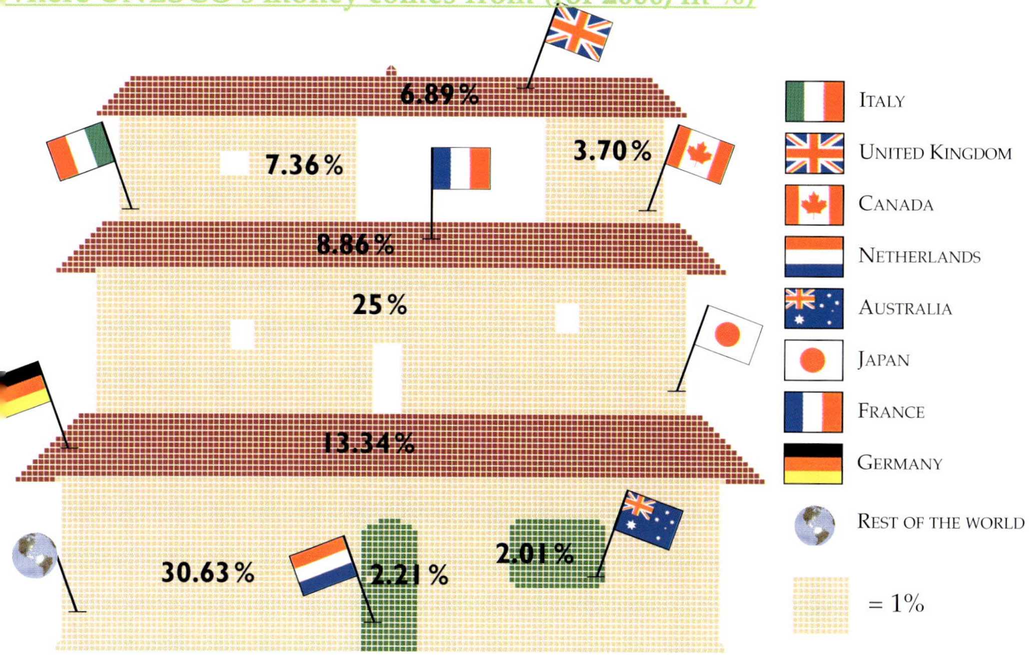
6.89 %
7.36 %
3.70 %
8.86 %
25 %
13.34 %
30.63 %
2.21 %
2.01 %
ITALY
UNITED KINGDOM
CANADA
NETHERLANDS
AUSTRALIA
JAPAN
FRANCE
GERMANY
REST OF THE WORLD
= 1%

How UNESCO spends its income (for 2000)

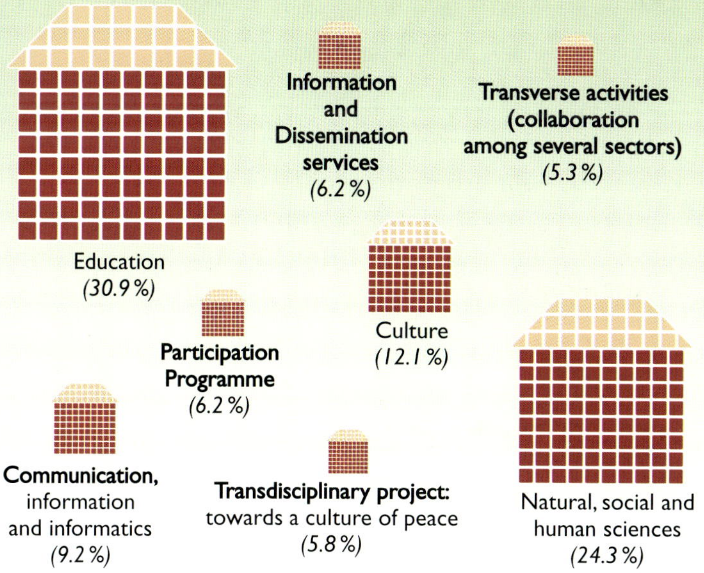
Education
(30.9 %)
Information and Dissemination services
(6.2 %)
Transverse activities (collaboration among several sectors)
(5.3 %)
Participation Programme
(6.2 %)
Culture
(12.1 %)
Communication, information and informatics
(9.2 %)
Transdisciplinary project: towards a culture of peace
(5.8 %)
Natural, social and human sciences
(24.3 %)

In 1984–1985, the departure of the United States, the United Kingdom and Singapore from UNESCO reduced the Organization's income by about 30%. This naturally obliged UNESCO to increase the contributions of the remaining member States and, at the same time, to introduce measures to economize on expenditure, notably by reducing the number of staff at the Organization.

UNESCO's five missions

The Constitution defines five major missions for UNESCO to undertake. They are:

● The Organization has a duty to undertake prospective *analysis forecasting**. It must try to anticipate the great upheavals which will affect societies and assess the future of education, science, culture and communication. In recent years, for example, UNESCO has been studying changes in the fields of knowledge and information brought about by the development of the World Wide Web (the Internet).

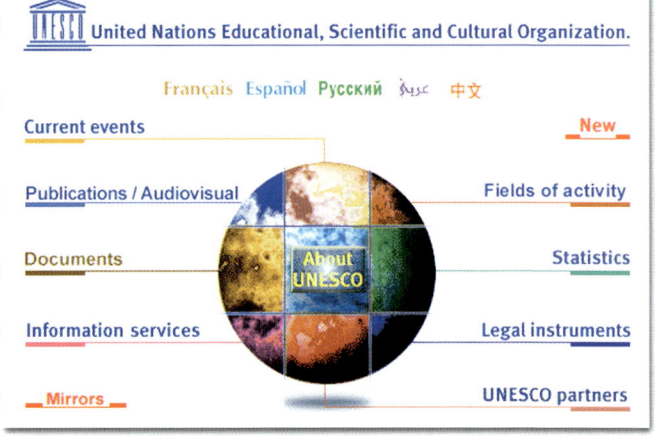

● By granting priority to *research, teaching and training*, UNESCO must ensure that scholars, teachers and students all over the world increase knowledge, and share it so that the greatest number of people can benefit with no one left out.

● UNESCO is called upon *to set standards*, or rather to create, modify and apply the rules of international law (universal laws, as it were, by which all countries must abide). This is why UNESCO is constantly making and adopting declarations, proclamations, recommendations, etc.

• UNESCO is expected to act in an *advisory capacity* to Member States, giving advice on national policy and development projects. In such instances, the Organization provides in 'technical co-operation' by co-ordinating major restoration work to save a monument, for example.

ANGKOR WAT, CAMBODIA

• UNESCO is a *forum* for exchange. It gathers and broadcasts information far and wide in its designated fields of competence: education, science, culture and communication. It does so by means of the written word and more and more through the medium of the new technologies. It organizes symposia, commissions reports and sees to it that specialists exchange ideas.

Did you know?

Eight out of ten people live in the developing countries.

FRANKFURT BOOK FAIR, GERMANY

UNESCO Activities

● *Education*

The scope of the activities pursued by UNESCO has evolved considerably over the years. At first, the Organization sought to rebuild education systems and, in Europe, to reopen museums and libraries whose collections had been destroyed or dispersed in the war. With the arrival of the new countries emerging from the old colonial period, however, UNESCO had to redefine its tasks. The pressing issue was how to endow the new countries with educational systems and library networks of their own.

In the 1960s, the Organization launched a worldwide programme to combat illiteracy. But the scale of the undertaking meant that the battle could not be won quickly. Thirty years later, in 1990, at a conference in Jomtien, Thailand, UNESCO and its partners made it their goal to reduce illiteracy in the world by 50% over the next decade.

In April 2000, the World Forum on Education for All held in Dakar, estimated that 880 million adults, or 20% of the world population, still lacks the rudiments of instruction that would enable them to read and write. UNESCO therefore pledged to enable all children everywhere to benefit from basic education by 2015. Today, UNESCO devotes almost one third of its resources to education (30.9% of the budget in 2000–2001) and has reaffirmed its priority commitment to basic learning for all. This will be one of the major programmes promoted by the Organization in the coming years. Education is the key to economic, political and social de-

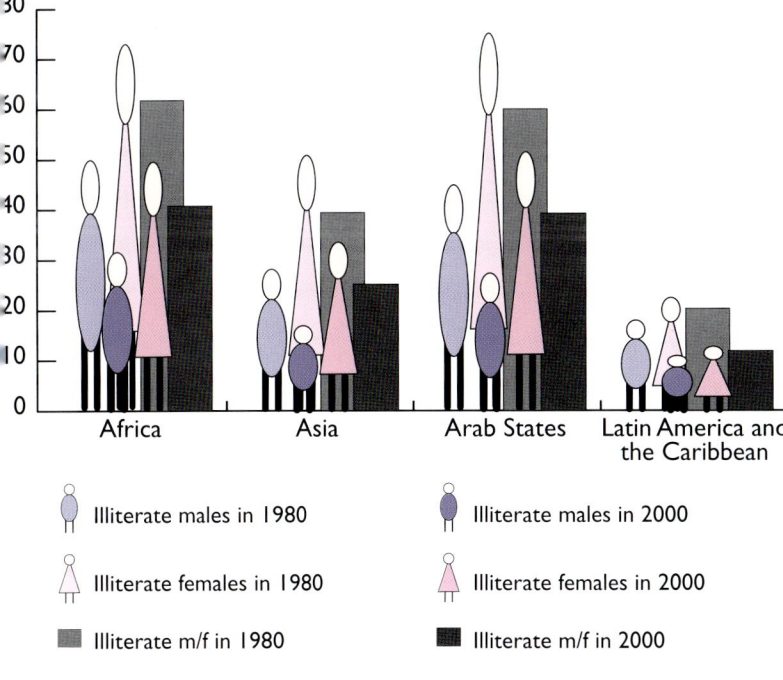

Changes in Adult illiteracy rates (aged 15 and over), 1980–2000 (in %)

Y-axis: 0, 10, 20, 30, 40, 50, 60, 70, 80

Categories: Africa, Asia, Arab States, Latin America and the Caribbean

Legend:
- Illiterate males in 1980
- Illiterate males in 2000
- Illiterate females in 1980
- Illiterate females in 2000
- Illiterate m/f in 1980
- Illiterate m/f in 2000

Did you know?

The number of children of school age who are not in school is steadily decreasing: 127 million in 1990, 113 million (20%) in 2001.

• *World Heritage* preservation*

UNESCO's actions on behalf of the preservation of the world heritage have undoubtedly been their most spectacular. Currently, the Organization is involved in protecting over 600 sites in different parts of the world deemed to be of 'exceptional universal value' on account of their historic, cultural, geographical or natural interest.

The natural sites on the World Heritage List have been chosen for their outstanding physical, biological and geological features, which together form exceptional areas from the point of view of science, the conservation of natural beauty or habitats for endangered vegetable or animal species.

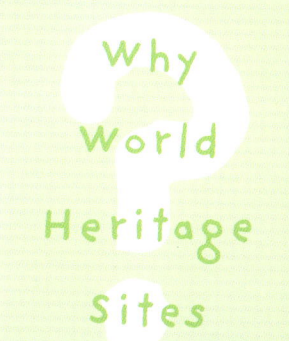

Why World Heritage Sites

BECAUSE they are spectacular.
BECAUSE they are testimonies of the past.
Because they are testimonies of endangered ways of life.
BECAUSE they provide shelter for threatened vegetable or animal species.
BECAUSE they contain rare geological formations.
BECAUSE they are unique.
BECAUSE they are artistic masterpieces.
BECAUSE they are at risk of being lost forever.
BECAUSE they belong to the whole world.

RECONSTRUCTION OF ABU SIMBEL TEMPLE, EGYPT

*Many French monuments and landscapes have been placed on the list of world heritage sites by UNESCO: Mont St. Michel and its Bay, Bourges Cathedral and Chartres Cathedral, the Park and Palace of Versailles, the Pont **du Gard and the Banks of the Seine, in Paris**.*

Several missions accomplished by the Organization in this field have aroused worldwide attention. From 1960 to 1965, there was the dismantling of the Nubian temple of Abu Simbel (Egypt) with reconstruction sixty metres above the original site, to prevent its being submerged by the rising waters of the Nile after the building of the Aswan Dam. In 1972, this was followed by another large-scale operation designed to restore the Buddhist temple of Borobudur, in Indonesia, which was threatened with collapse. More masterpieces saved with the help of UNESCO include the Great Wall (northern China), the Temples of Angkor (Cambodia), and the Old City of Dubrovnik (Croatia).

LE MONT SAINT MICHEL

BANKS OF THE SEINE, PARIS

On 1 January 2001, UNESCO's World Heritage List comprised 691 natural and cultural sites found in 122 countries. The most recent additions to this inventory include: the Loire Valley, the Historic Centres of the Cities of Bruges (Belgium) and Arequipa (Peru), the Castle of Elsinore, cherished by Hamlet (Denmark), the City of Verona, backdrop to the impassioned love of Romeo and Juliet (Italy) and the Island of Saint-Louis (Senegal).

THE MOSQUE IN DJENNÉ, MALI

In other parts of the world, the inventory includes: the Taj Mahal, the white marble tomb in Agra (India); the Park of Palenque strewn with Maya constructions (Mexico); the old towns of Djenné (Mali); the Iguazu National Park (Argentina); the ruins of the dead city of Petra (Jordan); the Great Barrier Reef (Australia); the Andean City of Potosí (Bolivia); the forbidden City of Beijing, the principal palace of the Ming and Qing emperors (China); the Galapagos Islands (Ecuador); the Moorish Palace of Alhambra in Granada (Spain); the Grand Canyon National Park (United States); the city of St. Petersburg (Russia); the Historic Centre of Rome (Italy); the cities of Fez, Meknès and Marrakesh (Morocco), etc.

In the name of world heritage protection, UNESCO has condemned as a 'crime against culture' the destruction of the ancient statues in Afghanistan in 2001, in particular the magnificent and well-known Buddhas of Bamyan, called 'anti-islamic' by the Taliban who dynamited them.

IMPERIAL PALACE, HUÉ, VIET NAM

OUALATA, MAURITANIA

Stealing works of art: museums strike back

STOLEN

Oil painting on copper with figures in a landscape symbolizing autumn, by Frans Francken II and Govaerts. On the back there may be a wax seal with the arms of the Marquis of Livois. Dimensions 25 x 42 cm.

Stolen from museum in Angers, France, on 6 September 1997. (Reference 39269/97, Interpol, The Hague).

Photo by courtesy of the ICPO–Interpol General Secretariat, Lyons (France)

THE 'STOLEN' PAGE IN THE INTERNATIONAL JOURNAL *MUSEUM*, A UNESCO PUBLICATION

UNESCO also strives to combat the theft of works of art from museums. It is sad that objects highly prized for their cultural value by the peoples who own them collectively and see them as witnesses of their past, should be stolen to enhance the collections of the few. The 1970 Convention on the Illicit Trade in Cultural Property marked a first step to define the lax in this respect. Even so, in 2000, the Organization considered that only 5–10% of stolen works were ever recovered. All in all, this is a steady drain on cultural life-blood.

• Spreading the word through representative works

In 1948 UNESCO launched a vast translation programme designed to acquaint the greatest number of readers with the most representative classical and contemporary writings of African, Creole, European, Ibero-American, Oceanian and Oriental cultures. In 1952, a Convention on the Protection of Intellectual Property was adopted under the auspices* of the Organization. The products of human intelligence and creativity should find their way to a large audience, but they must not be plundered or plagiarized: such works must be protected legally from pirated editions if creativity is to flower and benefit all gifted people and their cultures, while at the same time reaching as wide a readership as possible.

• The General History of Africa

Another ambitious project carried out by UN-ESCO was the writing and publishing of *General History of Africa*. Launched in the 1960s, this enterprise was completed in 1999. A total of eight volumes, were published. The publication of the volumes entitled *History of the Civilizations of Central Asia* was launched in 1992. A first version of the *History of the Cultural and Scientific Development of Mankind* was published from 1967 to 1969 (a second version, the *History of Mankind*, in seven volumes, is in press). Other history collections deal with Latin America and the Caribbean. These works allow readers to appreciate cultural riches which they may not otherwise have discovered.

POTTERY IN
OMAN

• The library of Alexandria

Since 1988, UNESCO has been helping Egypt to design and build a huge library in the city of Alexandria. It is hoped that this building, an enormous cylinder intended to evoke the rising sun, will re-create the spirit of the library which, according to tradition, was burned and razed by Caesar's armies in the first century B.C.

SCALE MODEL OF THE
PROPOSED NEW
LIBRARY OF
ALEXANDRIA

33

NOGAKU THEATRE, JAPAN

• *Protecting intangible heritage*

UNESCO also tries to preserve the oral and immaterial cultural heritage (customs, dances, oral traditions, performing arts, craft techniques) so that everyone may enjoy them. This heritage contains the vestiges of wonderful talent handed down from the past, but is often threatened with extinction by standardization*. To survive, it must be protected against the advancement of industrialization and globalization.

In 1949, UNESCO set up an International Music Council and, in 1961, launched its record collections dedicated to the traditional world music. At the same time, thanks to the Linguapax programme, the Organization embarked upon the safeguarding of the great variety of languages still spoken in the world today (from 5,000 to 6,000). About 1,000 of these are in danger of being lost in the next few years: the number of those who know them and speak them is so few, and these individuals are so elderly, that they can no longer be taught and handed down. Diversity represents an immense treasure-house of wealth; it must not be allowed to just fade away.

UNESCO takes an interest in all types of media. In particular, the Organization encourages large numbers of community radio stations in all parts of the world to transmit knowledge, promote dialogue and exchange and break the isolation of remote societies.

Did you know?

Africa has 216 radio stations and 60 television stations per 1,000 inhabitants, compared to 1,017 and 429 in the USA (1997 figures).

RADIO STATION *ANIMAS*, BOLIVIA   OUTDOOR RADIO INTERVIEW, MALI

34

What is intangible heritage?

FRAGILE TREASURES IN DANGER OF DISAPPEARING: skills and crafts, oral traditions, customs, dances.

THE GLUE THAT HOLDS COMMUNITIES TOGETHER: shared riches forge the identity of peoples and create powerful bonds (people understand one another and observe the same cultural habits).

THE BASES OF ARTISTIC AND CULTURAL DIVERSITY, THE REMEDY FOR UNIFORMITY: preserving this legacy is the best way to fight standardization. By making it known throughout the world, UNESCO helps to revitalize cultural life.

☀ *Scientific programmes*

UNESCO encourages scientific co-operation and, in particular, fair and sustainable development for everybody: we must leave our planet in good condition for the generations that will live after us. In 1957, a programme was launched to tackle the problem of deserts, also called arid regions. Three years later, the Intergovernmental Oceanographic Commission was set up, and a programme on the management of coastal zones was introduced. In 1978, UNESCO published the *Soil Map of the World.*

A SLUM
IN SOUTH AFRICA

ARID REGION
IN NIGER

UNESCO insists that the promotion of techniques or skills can be a means towards improving the living conditions of different categories of underprivileged populations. Since 1966, it has advocated the use of solar and wind* energy in regions where there is no electricity.

At the end of 2000, UNESCO decided to devote a significant part of its actions in the future to water resources and the protection of ecosystems.

WINDMILLS

SOLAR PANELS, ISRAEL

COLLECTING SAMPLES OF SEA WATER IN HAVANA, CUBA

Percentage of government expenditure used for scientific research
(% of gross national product)

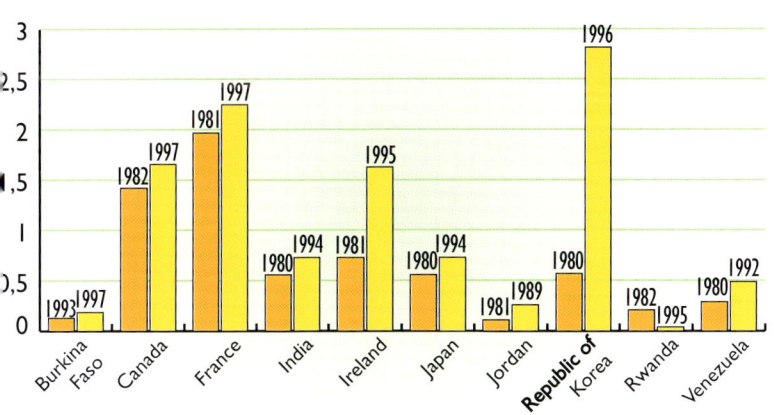

In general, expenditure increases at a regular rate, it can increase very sharply, which may indicate an economic take-off. Sometimes, it falls dramatically, which all too often means a war.

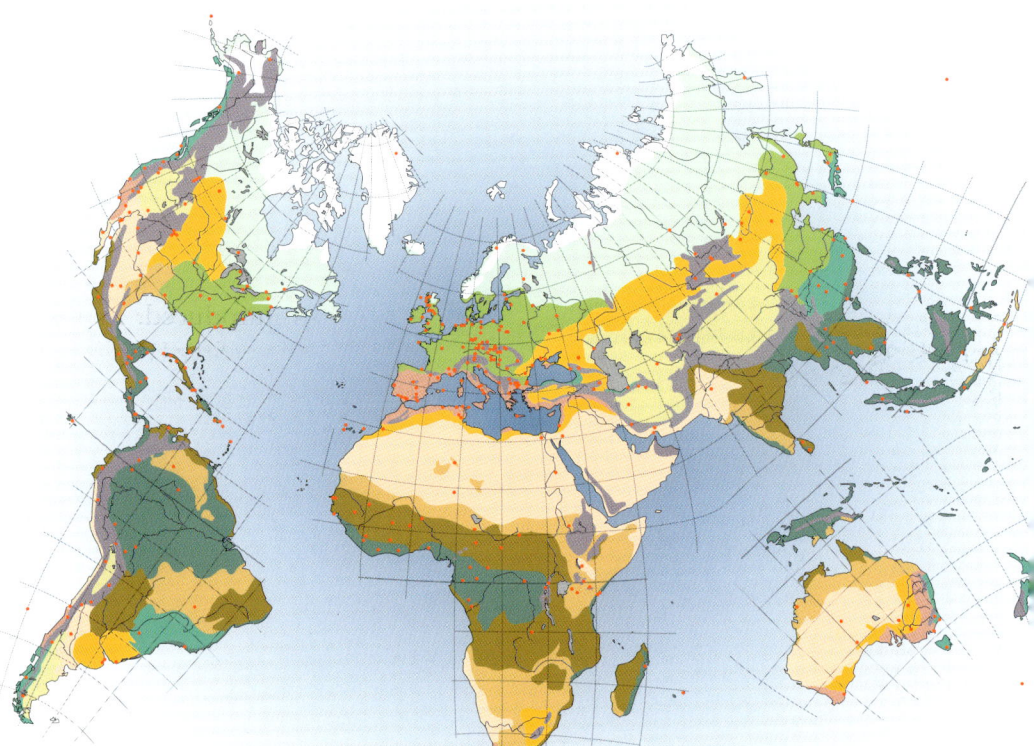

Throughout the 1970s and 1980s, a series of programmes were devoted to protecting the biosphere, which includes the entire biological habitat containing human beings, animals and plants (dry land, oceans, atmosphere, etc.). Such habitats are often fragile, but they are essential for the survival of the species.

The concept of biosphere reserves was the response to a big challenge: how can we preserve the immense diversity of plants, animals and micro-organisms that make up balanced ecosystems, while at the same time providing the resources needed for increasing economic development? In other words, how can we both use and save our natural biological resources?

The biosphere reserves make it possible to keep a watch on conservation and the stability of natural systems. They can be studied by scientists who see how they were used over the centuries, and how they are being used today. The data they provide – scientific, social and cultural statistics – can be collated and analysed and made available to everyone.

 TROPICAL HUMID FOREST

 SUB-TROPICAL AND TEMPERATE RAINFORESTS

 BOREAL NEEDLELEAF FORESTS OR WOODLANDS

 TROPICAL DRY OR DECIDUOUS FORESTS (INCLUDING MONSOON FORESTS)

 TEMPERATE AND SUB-POLAR BROADLEAF FORESTS OR WOODLANDS

 EVERGREEN SCLERO-PHYLLOUS FOREST, WOODLANDS OR SCRUB

 WARM DESERTS AND SEMI-DESERTS

 COLD WINTER (CONTINENTAL) DESERTS AND SEMI-DESERTS

 TUNDRA COMMUNITIES AND BARREN ARTIC DESERTS

 TROPICAL GRASSLANDS AND SAVANNAS

 TEMPERATE GRASSLAND

 MIXED MOUNTAIN AND HIGHLAND SYSTEMS

Water

A *UNIVERSAL NEED*: a person can die of thirst in three days. Our organism is made up of 70% of water. A tomato contains 90%. Each individual needs 5 litres of water per day for drinking and cooking, and 25 litres for personal hygiene.

FINITE RESOURCES: 97.5% of the water on the planet is salt-water, the remaining 2.5% cannot be fully utilized (70% is in the form of glaciers).

UNEQUAL EXPENDITURE: each member of a Canadian family uses, on an average, 350 litres of water a day, compared to 165 litres in Europe and 20 litres in Africa.

AN INDISPENSABLE RESOURCE FOR SUSTAINABLE DEVELOPMENT: agriculture is the highest water consumer (70%) but the water pumped from the fossil tables (very deep) cannot be renewed for future generations.

SOURCES OF SERIOUS CONFLICT: the great river basins of the world — where 40% of world population lives — are all used by several countries. The problem of water management (dams, pollution, canals to divert a portion of water supply) may become explosive issues in politics.

Did you know?

20% of world population has no access to clean drinking water, and 50% have no toilet facilities or bathrooms.

Awareness campaign against AIDS

UNESCO, in a very different field, has joined in the fight against AIDS, preparing pedagogical materials for educational planners, teachers and even children. In addition, the Organization approaches governments with a view to mobilizing decision-makers, urging them to set up awareness courses for teaching staff, women and community leaders.

MAKING OF AN
EDUCATIONAL FILM IN MALI

A moral code for scientists

For several years, UNESCO has been working towards endowing science and technology with a moral code: governments must find common ground in the prevention or restraining of excesses in scientific research, which may involve risky or debatable experiments. Accordingly, the Organization founded the International Bioethics* Committee (1993) and issued a declaration on the human genome* and human rights (1997). Mad scientists, serious discoveries deflected towards evil ends by wicked or unscrupulous politicians: these must remain the stuff of episodes in horror stories or science-fiction.

• Promoting and defending democracy

UNESCO strives to promote and defend democracy. The Organization played a prominent role, for example, in the struggle which obliged South Africa to abolish the discriminatory system of apartheid by launching a campaign to fight racial prejudice in 1949. UNESCO is also active in countries where democracy has yet to be introduced or needs support after a civil war or the fall of an authoritarian regime. The Organization intervened in Central America (El Salvador, 1991), in the countries of Eastern Europe (since the end of the 1990s), in Sub-Saharan Africa (Angola, Somalia), in certain parts of the former Yugoslavia by facilitating dialogue among the parties, and by organizing training courses on non-violent conflict resolution. Similarly, UNESCO is committed to fighting the discrimination against women and girls that still exists in many countries.

APARTHEID, SOUTH AFRICA

42

The challenges for the present and the future

CLEAN WATER IN SUFFICIENT QUANTITY FOR ALL:
ONE OF THE GREAT CHALLENGES OF THE 21ST CENTURY

UNESCO is an organization open to today's challenges, but the missions it seeks to accomplish are essentially the same: education for all, science at the service of development, conservation of the cultural and natural world heritage, human rights, peace among men, dialogue between cultures.

Over the past few decades, the world was carved up into broad sectors: on the one hand the East (the former Soviet block) and the West (Western countries) and on the other, the North (the industrialized countries) and the South (the developing countries). These divisions have now been made obsolete by globalization, yet the difference between rich and poor countries still subsists, while certain problems are more burning than ever: social injustice and inequality, the non-respect of different cultures, illiteracy, lack of schools and money for education, environmental pollution, and problems of access to the new communication technologies in the non-industrialized countries.

43

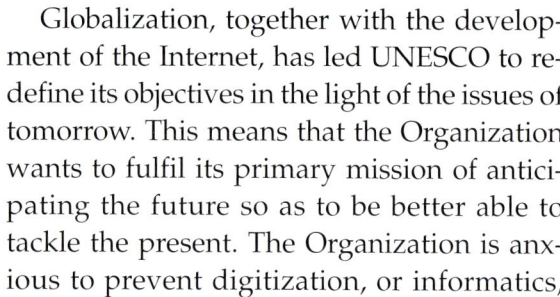

THE EDUCATION OF GIRL IS A POWERFUL LEVER IN DEVELOPMENT

Globalization, together with the development of the Internet, has led UNESCO to re-define its objectives in the light of the issues of tomorrow. This means that the Organization wants to fulfil its primary mission of anticipating the future so as to be better able to tackle the present. The Organization is anxious to prevent digitization, or informatics, from marginalizing whole populations with no access whatsoever to information and know-how because they are poor and their technical equipment is inadequate. This is what UNESCO calls 'globalization with a human face' to ensure a fairer distribution of knowledge.

UNESCO remains a place where all countries can come together in an attempt to find solutions so that, in a unified world, peoples may live in peace, each with its own traditions, language, way of thinking and being. And, in the face of that unification, UNESCO proclaims, more vigorously than ever, that culture is the fountain-head of all human activity.

LITTLE BY LITTLE, THE FIGHT AGAINST LAND DRAINAGE CONTINUES TO PUSH BACK THE DESERT

Globalization with a human face

FIGHTING POVERTY: 1.3 billion inhabitants of the planet live in utter destitution. UNESCO helps to devise means of development which take into account the way of life and the culture of each people. It favours approaches that assist populations in finding their own way out of poverty, through education, small grants, participation and the promotion of women.

Refusing to abandon whole populations with no access to the NEW COMMUNICATIONS AND INFORMATION TECHNOLOGIES

SAFEGUARDING THE CHANCES OF FUTURE GENERATIONS by meeting present needs, without compromising the capacity of succeeding generations to fill theirs. In terms of water, energy and the environment, for example, it is vital that today we learn to think of tomorrow.

Glossary

ANALYSIS FORECASTING. Research on the future of men and women, which makes it possible to produce certain forecasts.

APARTHEID. System of racial segregation applied to all aspects of life (housing, work, education, services, etc.) in total violation of human rights.

ASSOCIATE MEMBERS. Territories which are not themselves directly responsible for control of their foreign relations. They have the same rights as the other States, with two exceptions: they do not vote and cannot sit at the Council.

AUSPICES. Patronage, protection, support.

BIOETHICS. Ethics applied to research in life sciences, and to their applications and social and human consequences.

ECOSYSTEMS. A biological community of interacting living organisms and the physical environment in which they live and evolve.

FINANCIAL BACKER. Person or institution who provides capital or finance.

GENOME. Set of chromosomes of a species.

HERITAGE. A nation's historic buildings, countryside, monuments, inherited from previous generations.

NGO. Nongovernmental organizations are private associations not dependant on States but able to accept subsidies. They are active in various fields: human right, health, education and environment among others.

SOLAR AND WIND ENERGY. Renewable, non-polluting forms of energy, generated from the sun and wind.

STANDARDIZATION. Everything conforms to the same model.

So, what can I do?

◈ Learn about human rights and children's rights and talk about them everywhere.

◈ If I am in France, pay a visit to UNESCO.

◈ Talk to the teachers about the system of Associated Schools.

◈ Set up a UNESCO club in my school or my college.

◈ Visit the World Heritage sites in my region, and suggest to my school that we should study them as a group.

◈ Be interested in the protection of the environment, try to pollute it as little as possible and learn how to keep it clean.

Useful addresses

UNESCO
7, Place de Fontenoy
75007 Paris
Tel.: 01 45 68 10 00
Fax: 01 45 67 16 90
Website: www.unesco.org

◈

UK UNESCO
(which manages the network of UK UNESCO Clubs)
The British Council
10 Spring Gardens
London SW1A 2BN
Telephone: 020 7389 4687
Fax: 020 7389 4497

Table of Contents

Photos © UNESCO
Photography: E. Barrios (pp. 7, 44/3), N. Burke (pp. 4, 14/1-3-4, 15/2),
R. Carrington (pp. 36/1, 42), M. Claude (pp. 13, 14/2, 15/1-3-4), D. Decker (p. 26/3),
P. Donnaint (p. 36/2), F. Dunouau (p. 6), I. Forbes (pp. 15/5, 29/2, 30/4),
A. Gillette (p. 33/1), A. Hossain (p. 26/1), S. Janah (p. 35/2), A. Jonquières (p. 34/2),
N. Levinthal (p. 11), P. Lissac (p. 44/1), A. Lopez (p. 37/2), G. Malempré (p. 25/1-2),
B. Nantet (p. 40/2), Nenadovic (p. 30/2), S. Robert (p. 31/3),
D. Roger (pp. 20, 21/1-3, 22, 25/3, 29/1, 30/1, 32/2, 34/3, 40/3, 41, 43, 44/2),
N. Saunier (p. 37/1), A. Snoheta (p. 33/2-3), Tandem (p. 21/2), H. Uluk (p. 26/2),
UNESCO (pp. 8, 16, 34/1, 35/1-3-4), A. N. Vorontzoff (p. 31/1-2).

Photos © BIOS
Photography: F. Bruemmer (p. 39/11), X. Eichaker (p. 39/7), H. Klein (p. 39/12),
F. Lasserre (p. 39/10), B. Lundberg (p. 39/9), B. Marcon (p. 39/2),
J. Mingorance Gutierez (p. 39/6), Seitre (p. 39/3), P. Vaucoulon (p. 39/4),
P. Weimann (p. 39/1).

Photo p. 39/8 © WWF, BIOS. Photography: F. Polking.
Photo p. 39/5 © ONF. Photography: J-P. Chasseau.
Photo p. 40/1 © Agence de l'eau Seine-Normandie. Photography: D. Guichard.

◈

Layout: Eric Frogé
Illustrations: Pascale Collange

◈

Printed in Spain by Sagrafic, Barcelona – November 2001
UNESCO Publishing